FUSION

GET OUTDOORS

Go Paddling!

by Meghan Gottschall

BEARPORT
PUBLISHING

Minneapolis, Minnesota

President: Jen Jenson
Director of Product Development: Spencer Brinker
Senior Editor: Allison Juda
Designer: Colin O'Dea

Library of Congress Cataloging-in-Publication Data

Names: Gottschall, Meghan, author.
Title: Go paddling! / by Meghan Gottschall.
Description: Fusion books. | Minneapolis, Minnesota : Bearport Publishing
Company, [2022] | Series: Get outdoors | Includes bibliographical references and index.
Identifiers: LCCN 2021002678 (print) | LCCN 2021002679 (ebook) | ISBN 9781647479695 (library binding) |
    ISBN 9781647479763 (paperback) | ISBN 9781647479831 (ebook)
Subjects: LCSH: Canoes and canoeing--Juvenile literature. |
Kayaking--Juvenile literature. | Outdoor recreation--Juvenile literature.
Classification: LCC GV784.3 .G68 2022 (print) | LCC GV784.3 (ebook) | DDC 797.122--dc23
LC record available at https://lccn.loc.gov/2021002678
LC ebook record available at https://lccn.loc.gov/2021002679

For more information, write to Bearport Publishing, 5357 Penn Avenue South, Minneapolis, MN 55419. Printed in the United States of America.

CONTENTS

A PADDLING ADVENTURE

Spending your day on the water can be fun. Grab your life jacket. We're going on a paddling adventure!

Make sure your life jacket is buckled and snug.

Hi, I'm Rory Raccoon, and I love to GET OUTDOORS!

Paddling means using a paddle to help you move your boat through the water. You can paddle in a kayak, a raft, or a canoe. It's up to you!

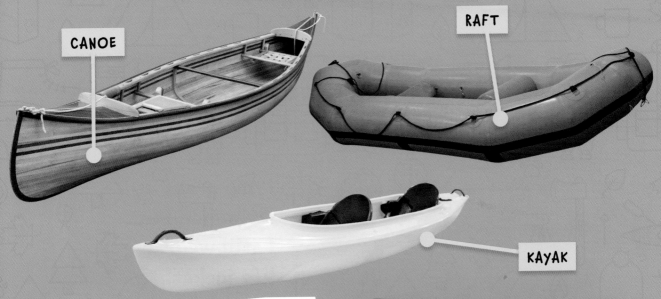

CANOE

RAFT

KAYAK

Some people also head to the water with a paddleboard. They sit, kneel, or stand as they paddle.

PADDLEBOARD

5

WHAT TO WEAR

What should you wear for your day on the water? First, you need a life jacket. Be sure to wear one every time you're on a boat.

I'm a great swimmer, but I still wear a life jacket!

6

Being around water means you could get wet. You may want to wear a swimsuit. Or you might just wear clothes that can dry quickly. Bring **layers** in case the weather changes.

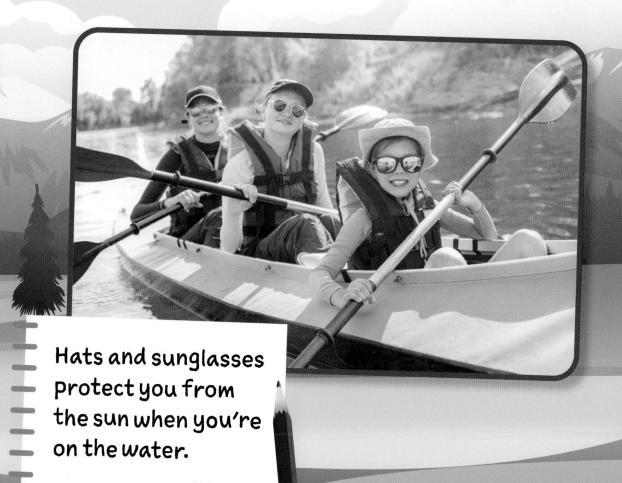

Hats and sunglasses protect you from the sun when you're on the water.

GETTING YOUR GEAR

The most important piece of paddling gear is your paddle, of course! Choose one that's the right size for you. It should not be too long or too heavy for you to move easily.

BLADE

Grab your kayak paddle right here!

A kayak paddle has a **blade** on each end. Hold the paddle in the middle with both hands.

Canoe and raft paddles are shorter and have one blade. You can put one hand where the blade meets the shaft. This place is called the throat. Place your other hand on the grip at the other end of the shaft.

BLADE

SHAFT

THROAT

GRIP

TIP

Look at all the names for different parts of a paddle!

ALL ABOUT BOATS

Canoes are small, thin boats that are open on top. They often have benches to sit on. Usually two or more people can paddle in a canoe.

Kayaks are shaped a lot like canoes but have closed **decks**. Your legs go inside the boat. Often, kayaks have room for only one person.

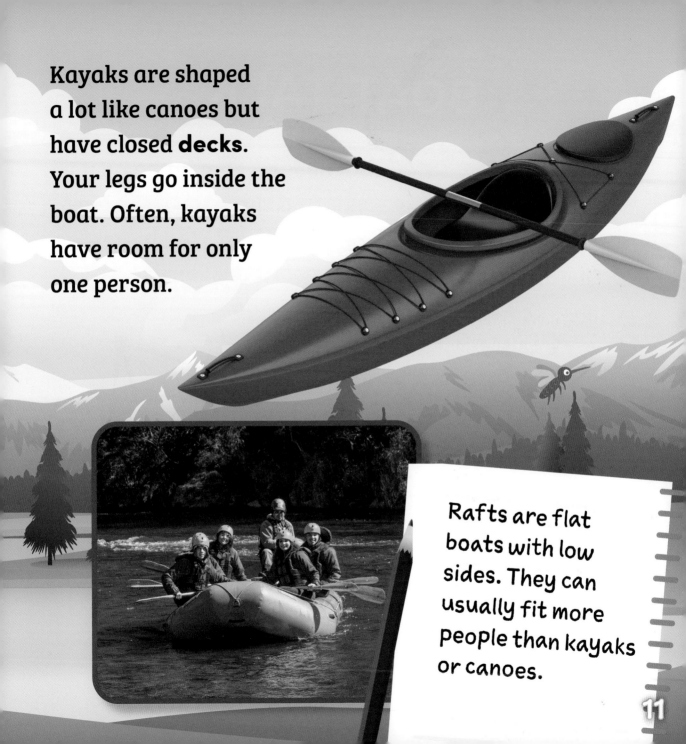

Rafts are flat boats with low sides. They can usually fit more people than kayaks or canoes.

BOAT TALK

All aboard! Hop in the **port** side and climb up to the bow. Wait . . . what? We'd better learn our boat words before we go.

On a boat, you don't say left or right. Say **starboard** for the right side of the boat.

The front of the boat is called the bow.

Use port for the left side of a boat.

STAYING AFLOAT

Kayaks and canoes can tip over if you are not careful. There are some good places to sit when you're first learning to paddle. The middle or front seats of a canoe are good for your first trip. An adult can sit behind you.

Life jackets keep us safe if we fall into the water.

You can keep **stable** by staying in your spot. Don't stand up in a boat. Try not to lean too far to either side.

Try a two-person kayak with an adult when you first start out.

GRAB YOUR PADDLE

Now it's time to get moving. Lower the paddle into the water in front of you. Pull the blade through the water from front to back. Then, pick up the paddle and move it through the air to the front and do it all again.

Paddling is hard work. You have to be strong!

One of the oldest paddles ever found is more than 8,000 years old.

The person paddling in the stern **steers** the boat. They paddle on the right side to turn left. They paddle on the left side to turn right.

When both people paddle on the same side, the boat will turn.

YOUR FIRST TIME OUT

What should you keep in mind for your first paddling trip? Watch out for weeds! It's easy to get stuck if you run into seaweed or other water plants. If there's wind, paddle across it rather than directly into it.

Pick short trips at first. You'll need to have enough **energy** to paddle back to shore.

Choose a place with calm water. This is also called flat water. **Whitewater** is fast-moving water. Some people take kayaks, canoes, or rafts on whitewater. But this takes lots of practice.

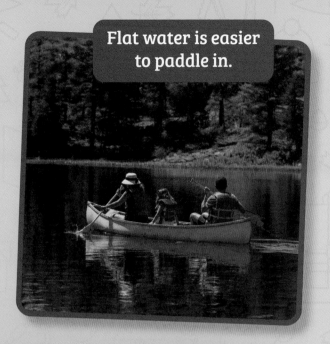

Flat water is easier to paddle in.

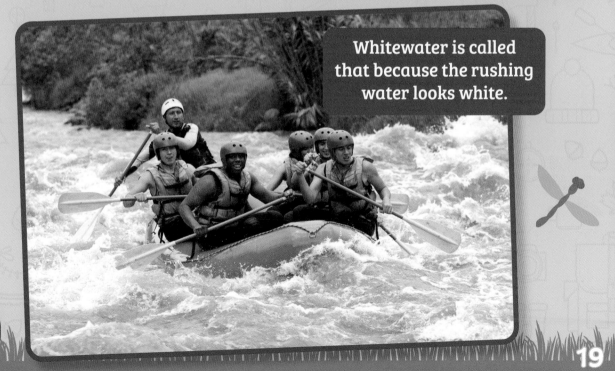

Whitewater is called that because the rushing water looks white.

WISE ON THE WATER

Paddling is a great way to see nature. Be on the lookout for fish, birds, and other animals. Give **wildlife** plenty of space. This will keep everyone safe.

Herons are birds that wade in the water and eat fish.

Make sure you don't **disturb** any animal homes you come across. You can look at nests or beaver dams from a distance.

Beavers build dams from rocks, sticks, branches, and mud.

Never throw trash in the water! Make sure you take it away with you when you're done with your paddling trip.

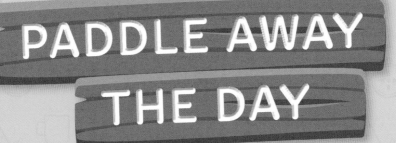

PADDLE AWAY THE DAY

There's nothing like spending a beautiful day outdoors. And being on the water makes it even better. Paddling can be a lot of work, but it's so fun to do with family and friends. You never know what you might see in a river or on a lake.

23

GLOSSARY

blade the flat part of a paddle that is used to push water

decks the floors of ships or boats

disturb to bother someone or something

energy the power needed by all living things to grow and stay alive

layers many levels of something, such as clothing, lying one over another

port the left side of a boat

stable firm and steady

starboard the right side of a boat

steers controls the direction of a vehicle or boat

whitewater water in a river that is moving very fast

wildlife wild animals living in their natural setting

INDEX